ELFiS

A CHRISTMAS TALE

Written by Alan Katz and Pete Fornatale

Illustrated by Dani Jones

PSS!

PRICE STERN SLOAN

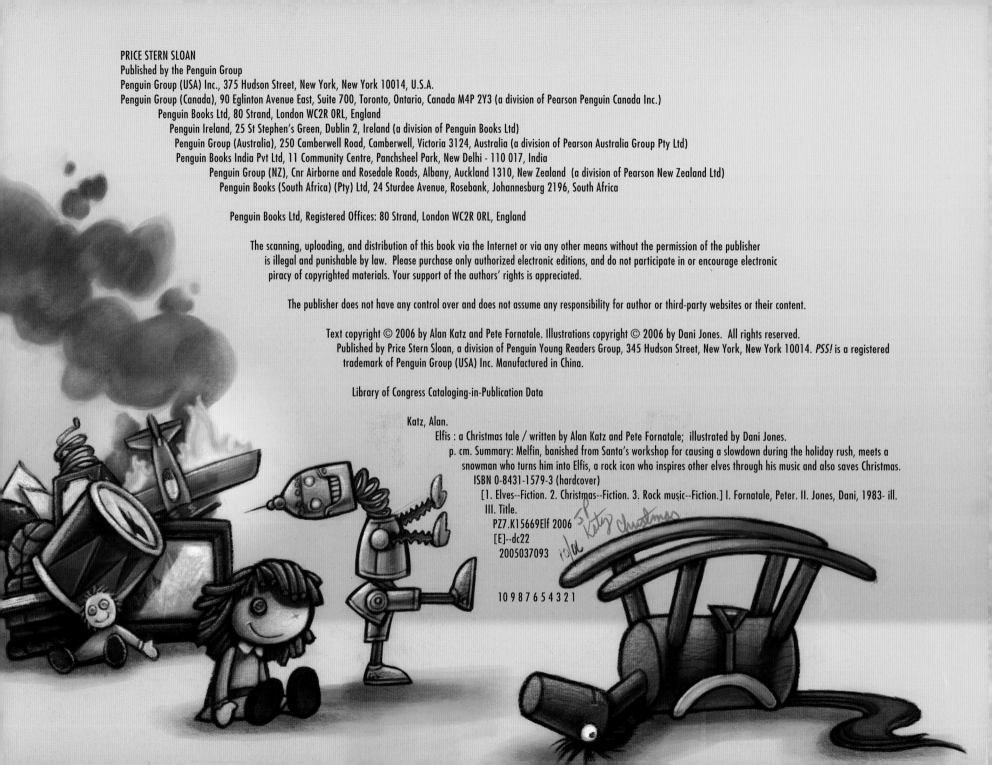

PRICE STERN SLOAN
Published by the Penguin Group
Penguin Group (USA) Inc., 375 Hudson Street, New York, New York 10014, U.S.A.
Penguin Group (Canada), 90 Eglinton Avenue East, Suite 700, Toronto, Ontario, Canada M4P 2Y3 (a division of Pearson Penguin Canada Inc.)
Penguin Books Ltd, 80 Strand, London WC2R 0RL, England
Penguin Ireland, 25 St Stephen's Green, Dublin 2, Ireland (a division of Penguin Books Ltd)
Penguin Group (Australia), 250 Camberwell Road, Camberwell, Victoria 3124, Australia (a division of Pearson Australia Group Pty Ltd)
Penguin Books India Pvt Ltd, 11 Community Centre, Panchsheel Park, New Delhi - 110 017, India
Penguin Group (NZ), Cnr Airborne and Rosedale Roads, Albany, Auckland 1310, New Zealand (a division of Pearson New Zealand Ltd)
Penguin Books (South Africa) (Pty) Ltd, 24 Sturdee Avenue, Rosebank, Johannesburg 2196, South Africa

Penguin Books Ltd, Registered Offices: 80 Strand, London WC2R 0RL, England

Library of Congress Cataloging-in-Publication Data

Katz, Alan.
    Elfis : a Christmas tale / written by Alan Katz and Pete Fornatale; illustrated by Dani Jones.
        p. cm. Summary: Melfin, banished from Santa's workshop for causing a slowdown during the holiday rush, meets a
    snowman who turns him into Elfis, a rock icon who inspires other elves through his music and also saves Christmas.
        ISBN 0-8431-1579-3 (hardcover)
        [1. Elves--Fiction. 2. Christmas--Fiction. 3. Rock music--Fiction.] I. Fornatale, Peter. II. Jones, Dani, 1983- ill.
    III. Title.
    PZ7.K15669Elf 2006
    [E]--dc22
    2005037093

    10 9 8 7 6 5 4 3 2 1

To Miss Joy, for sharing the joys of reading.—AK

For the precious gift of imagination.—PF

To my parents, for their patience, faith, encouragement, and visits.—DJ

It was Christmas Eve, and all was not well at the old North Pole. The letters from kids were piling up faster than the elves could possibly make the toys. And even after Spiffy and Fluffy and Zippy and Miltie had gone through the millions of letters and pulled out all the duplicates (Roger Noonan, stop writing hundreds of letters to Santa—you're NOT getting a pet zebra!), the brightly flashing Toyometer frantically told the sad story:

TWO DAYS' WORTH OF TOYS TO MAKE! ONLY ONE DAY BEFORE CHRISTMAS!

With little time to spare, *rush, rush, rush* were the words
on everyone's lips.
Elves were huffing.
Elves were puffing.
Elves were building playthings faster than
ever before.
All except one…

TWO DAYS WORTH OF TOYS TO MAKE! ONLY ONE DAY BEFORE CHRISTMAS!

MELFIN.

Now when things were going smoothly in the workshop, Melfin the Elf was the one who tested all of the freshly made toys. In fact, if you see a tag attached to one of your toys that says, "Tested by # ½," that was Melfin.

But when Christmas got closer and things got really hectic, Melfin was overexcited, overenthusiastic, and overwhelmed…suddenly all thumbs and confusion. This close to the big day, Melfin was like a pint-sized, pressurized, personal predicament…which is not easy to say, and not easy to be. The sad truth was, Melfin was breaking more toys than the other elves were making.

And this was no year for that to be happening.

With a stack of busted toys behind him, Melfin was testing a brand-new guitar. He tugged at the strings a little too hard, and the instrument flew out of his hands and headed directly toward the stomach of kindly Mr. Knox, Santa's workshop supervisor.

With the wind knocked out of him, Mr. Knox gasped exasperatedly, "Melfin! Get out! You're messing things up! Slowing things down! We're manufacturing...you're manu*fracturing*! You must leave the workshop at once and take this sorry excuse for a guitar with you!"

"But... but..."

"No buts about it! The only 'butt' I want is yours...
out of here! Now good-bye!"

The next sound the pleading elf heard was...

SLAM!

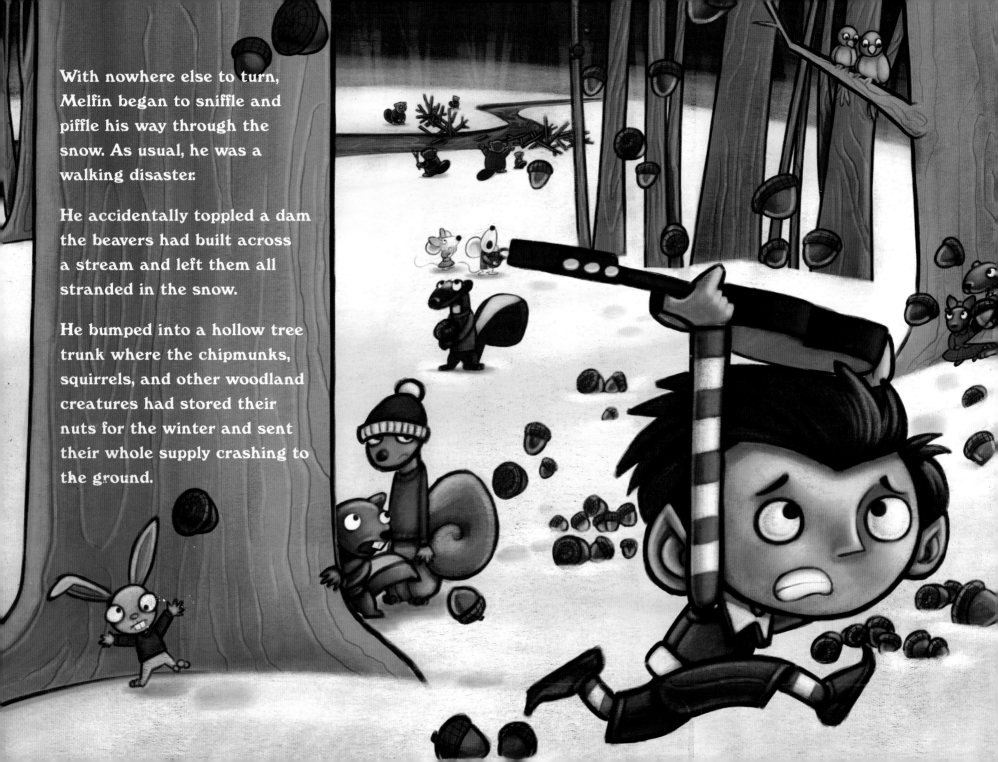

With nowhere else to turn, Melfin began to sniffle and piffle his way through the snow. As usual, he was a walking disaster.

He accidentally toppled a dam the beavers had built across a stream and left them all stranded in the snow.

He bumped into a hollow tree trunk where the chipmunks, squirrels, and other woodland creatures had stored their nuts for the winter and sent their whole supply crashing to the ground.

And perhaps worst of all, he stumbled and tumbled and knocked down the fence holding the reindeer... and they zipped away in all directions (especially Donner, who took off like a comet, and Comet, who for some reason took off like a dancer).

Too tired to continue, Melfin paused to sit on a tree stump next to a weathered but cheerful-looking snowman.

Feeling very sorry for himself, Melfin exclaimed to no one in particular, "I…I'm not such a bad guy. I tried hard. I just wish Mr. Knox could see I have a good soul!"

As his final word hung in the freezing night air, a strange stirring occurred! The wind howled! The sky poured down a blizzard of snow…in every color of the rainbow!

"Did you say *soul?*" a voice asked.

"Wh-who said that?"

"Me," the snowman answered, suddenly coming to life.

"Wh-who are you?"

"They call me the hardest-working man in snow business…
the boss of blizzards…and your soul brother number one!"
the snowman exclaimed.
"I'm here to put the *elf* back in 'believe in yours*elf*!'"

"But maybe Mr. Knox was right," Melfin said.
"After all, look at this guitar! It looks more like
a snow shovel than a musical instrument!"

The snowman called out, "Melfin, it's time for the world to see who you really are on the inside. It's time to start rockin' and rollin' your troubles away. You've got to believe in yourself, elf!"

"Okay, Mr. Snowman. But how?"

"It's easy, my main man. I mean, my main elf. When next on that guitar you strum, something magical you'll become!"

Melfin picked up the guitar, gave it a half-hearted pluck, and...

In a *ZAP-FLASH-KAPOW*, Melfin began spinning like a top in the snow!

As Melfin spun, the snowman added for good measure, "Twice the toys in half the time, with a rockin' beat and a magic rhyme!"

When the little guy stopped spinning, he was poor little Melfin no more. Instead, he was the king of rock 'n' roll at the old North Pole...he was...

Repeating to himself, "Twice the toys in half the time, twice the toys in half the time…" he suddenly knew what he had to do.

"Wow, that's it! Thanks, Mr. Snowman, and Merry Christmas!" Elfis exclaimed.

With his work done, the snowman was back to being…just a snowman. (Although if you looked really closely, you could see a wider smile than he'd had before!)

Elfis had no time to lose. With his brand-new shiny guitar in hand, he headed back to the workshop. But the beavers were just starting to rebuild the dam and Elfis couldn't get across.

So he started singing…

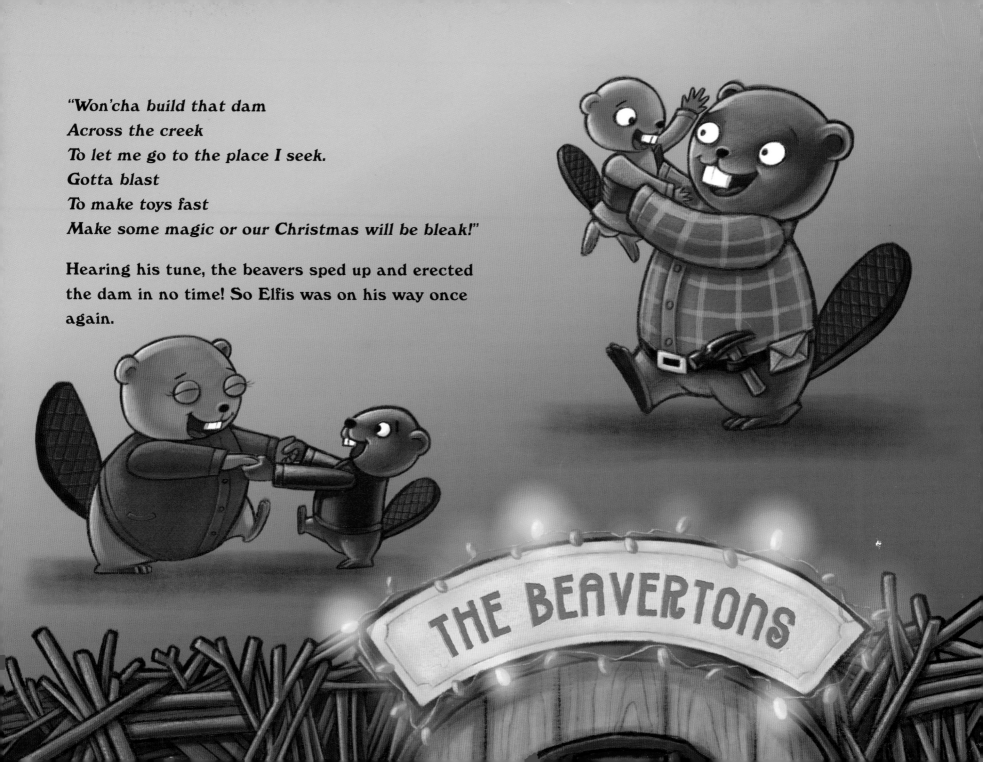

"Won'cha build that dam
Across the creek
To let me go to the place I seek.
Gotta blast
To make toys fast
Make some magic or our Christmas will be bleak!"

Hearing his tune, the beavers sped up and erected
the dam in no time! So Elfis was on his way once
again.

THE BEAVERTONS

But then he passed the chipmunks and squirrels, ever so slowly trying to get their winter's worth of nuts back into the hollow tree.

So Elfis sang…

"Well, bless my soul and woe is me,
You gotta get those nuts back into that tree.
So, critters, shake your tails,
Don't stand and shrug,
Let's all move
An' pick 'em up!
Mm, mm, oh yeah, yeah
Let's pick 'em up!"

Cheered by Elfis's song, the critters filled their tree
quickly, and Elfis rocked on toward the workshop.

But just before he got there,
he saw the empty reindeer pen.

So Elfis sang...

"Well since the reindeer left me,
They found a new place to dwell.
But now we need them back again
To serve the children well.
Hey, if you got shoo'd off, Rudolph,
No time to be stupid, Cupid,
Let's all go groove to the sleigh bell!"

And soon the reindeer scampered back from
every direction, ready for their big night.

Finally, Elfis reached the workshop. He peered into the window and checked the trusty Toyometer.

He saw that toy-making was at an all-time low. The Toyometer was flashing:

YOUR LITTLE BEHINDS ARE A LOT BEHIND! YOU'RE NEVER GOING TO MAKE IT!

TOYOMETER

YOUR LITTLE BEHINDS ARE A LOT BEHIND! YOU'RE NEVER GOING TO MAKE IT!

What's more, he saw that all his friends were sad at a time when they should've been full of joy!

"Sniff...it's just no fun around here since Knox threw him out!"

"Yeah, it's hard to keep my mind on these toys, knowing the poor little guy's out there in the snow somewhere..."

Elfis had no time to lose. He burst into the workshop and twanged a happy note on his guitar. Everyone looked up...and listened carefully as he sang the following, to a happy rock 'n' roll beat...

"Build one for little Bobby,
Two for pretty Sue,
Three for all the triplets,
We've got lotsa work to do!
Now won't you...step up that toy makin', oooh.
If we all just work together,
We can finish up on time, yeah, that's true!"

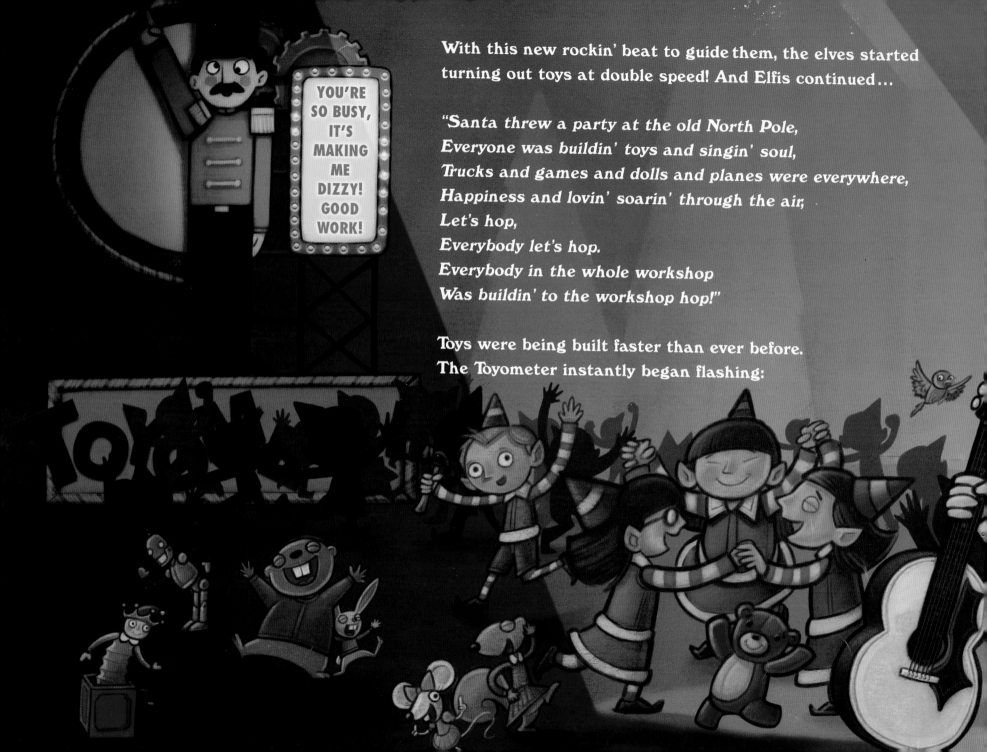

YOU'RE SO BUSY, IT'S MAKING ME DIZZY! GOOD WORK!

With this new rockin' beat to guide them, the elves started turning out toys at double speed! And Elfis continued...

"Santa threw a party at the old North Pole,
Everyone was buildin' toys and singin' soul,
Trucks and games and dolls and planes were everywhere,
Happiness and lovin' soarin' through the air,
Let's hop,
Everybody let's hop.
Everybody in the whole workshop
Was buildin' to the workshop hop!"

Toys were being built faster than ever before.
The Toyometer instantly began flashing:

YOU'RE SO BUSY, IT'S MAKING ME DIZZY! GOOD WORK!

Elfis kept strumming. The toy-makers were humming. And the stack of letters grew smaller and smaller and smaller as the stack of toys grew taller and taller and taller. And in no time at all, the Toyometer declared:

GIVE THAT GUY A STANDING O—THE TOYS ARE DONE AND SET TO GO!

Everyone in the place cheered and surrounded Elfis to show their appreciation for his rockin' beat. And the happiest of all was Mr. Knox, who shook Elfis's hand and said, "You're just what we needed around here. We couldn't have made it without you!"

That's when Elfis paused, smiled, and suddenly began his magical spin. Then...

...in a flash, he changed back into Melfin and said, *"That's exactly what I was trying to tell you!"*

Everyone gasped at the changeover—first in disbelief, then in delight!
Elfis, or rather, Melfin, had saved the toy-making effort! He was the
hero of the day.

As they continued to salute him, a booming voice was heard. "Melfin," the voice said, "your rockin' and rollin' beat helped the elves make more toys than ever before. But now, I've got the big job of delivering them all!"

"S-Santa?" Melfin asked.

"Right," Santa answered him. "And if I'm going to deliver a record number of toys, I'm going to need a boost, too! Would you please come with me and turn your toy-making beat into a toy-delivering beat?"

WHIRR! SPIN! FLASH! It was Elfis once again!

"You bet, Santa!" exclaimed Elfis. "Glad to! We've got a lot of givin' to do!"

And with that, they were set for their Christmas Eve ride…to get the whole world rockin' and rollin' together. As everyone gathered around the sleigh, Elfis jumped to the tippy-top of the toy bag and sang for all to hear:

"You'll have a great Christmas, I promise,
Every Paul, Sean, Jane, and Thomas.
Do like this little elf,
Just believe in yourself,
And you'll have a great, great, great,
great Christmas!"